DISHING IT UP Disney STYLE

A Cookbook for Families with Type 1 Diabetes

EDITIONS
NEW YORK

As a registered dietitian and certified diabetes educator working with kids who have diabetes and their families, I know that meal planning is an important part of diabetes management. I also know that mealtime should be fun for the whole family, but sometimes it's hard to get everyone together around the table. Why? Because it can be difficult to find dishes that suit the nutritional needs—and tastes!—of the entire household.

With this delightful Disney cookbook as a guide, moms, dads, and kids can rediscover how much fun it is to explore in the kitchen—while making meals that are both wholesome and delicious! The recipes in this cookbook are based on sound nutritional recommendations from the American Dietetic Association and the American Diabetes Association. They have been selected to provide options that are low in added sugar, high in fiber, and low in fat—but never lacking in taste!

While there is no one specific meal plan that fits all families, this cookbook includes a wide variety of recipes that can be good choices for anyone with type 1 diabetes. The simple step-by-step instructions are easy to follow, and Disney characters suggest tips for getting kids into the mix. Princesses, Lost Boys, piglets, and man-cubs can get involved preparing these delicious dishes that are just as much fun to eat as they are to make!

Nutritional analysis was provided by the Diabetes Care and Education Practice Group of the American Dietetic Association, with the expertise of Stefanie Leniszewski, MS, RD, CD, CDE, using DINE Healthy 7 software (http://www.dinesystems.com). For each recipe, the following information is included: serving size; servings per recipe; calories; total fat; total carbohydrate and carbohydrate choices (for those individuals who count grams of carbohydrates, as well as those who count carbohydrate choices); fiber; and protein.

For those with celiac disease, the gluten-free recipes are identified, and some recipes include notes indicating how they can be prepared in a gluten-free way. As always, all ingredients should be thoroughly checked for gluten as differences can occur between brands.

Now that the guesswork has been taken out of meal planning and nutrition calculation, it's time to enjoy cooking with the whole family!

Amy Hess Fischl, MS, RD, LDN, BC-ADM, CDE
Chair, Diabetes Care and Education Practice Group of the American Dietetic Association
2011–2012

* Photographs may contain additional food items or a different serving size than reflected in the nutritional analysis.

Table of Contents

Breakfast

Serving: ¾ cup
Calories: 124
Total Fat: 0g
Total Carbohydrate: 25g
Fiber: 2g
Protein: 5g
Carbohydrate Choice: 1 ½

Gluten-free note: use gluten-free yogurt.

Coco's
Banana Smoothie

Ingredients

1 frozen banana
½ cup nonfat yogurt
½ cup fresh orange juice
¼ cup blueberries, washed

Instructions

1. Combine all ingredients in a blender and blend until smooth.

Coco's Tip: Bananas have such appeal! Little ones can peel their bananas and measure out the orange juice.

Mickey's
No-Cook Muesli

Serving: about ⅓ cup muesli
   with ¼ cup berries
Calories: 270
Total Fat: 14g
Total Carbohydrate: 26g
Fiber: 5g
Protein: 11g
Carbohydrate Choice: 1 ½

Gluten-free note: prepare
with gluten-free oats.

Ingredients

1 cup plain nonfat yogurt
1 cup quick oats
½ cup whole nuts, such as almonds,
   walnuts, or pecans
1 tablespoon flaxseed meal (optional)
1 tablespoon maple syrup or honey
1 cup fresh berries

Instructions

1. In a blender, combine the yogurt, oats, nuts, flaxseed meal, and maple syrup or honey.
2. Blend until the oats and nuts are in small pieces (about 30 seconds), then divide the muesli among four bowls and top with the berries. Or blend ½ cup of berries with the muesli and garnish with the rest.

Mickey's Tip: It's important to eat breakfast, especially when you get up early to go fishing with your faithful pup! Parents should supervise while using the blender, but encourage kids to measure out the ingredients and wash the berries.

Snow White's
Crunchy Homemade Granola

Ingredients

4 cups rolled oats
1 cup wheat germ
1 cup chopped walnuts or slivered almonds
½ cup sesame seeds
¼ cup brown sugar
1 teaspoon cinnamon
¼ teaspoon salt

⅓ cup vegetable oil
⅓ cup honey
⅓ cup water
1 (6-ounce) package dried sweetened cranberries or other dried fruits, such as cherries, raisins, pineapple, or papaya

Instructions

1. Heat the oven to 300°F. In a large mixing bowl, stir together the oats, wheat germ, nuts, sesame seeds, brown sugar, cinnamon, and salt.
2. Make a well in the dry ingredients and add the oil, honey, and water. Toss the mixture until the ingredients are well combined, then spread it evenly on a cookie sheet.
3. Bake the granola for 40 minutes or until lightly browned, stirring every 10 minutes to keep the mixture from sticking. Let it cool completely, then stir in the cranberries or dried fruit.

Serving: ½ cup
Calories: 325
Total Fat: 16g
Total Carbohydrate: 38g
Fiber: 6g
Protein: 7g
Carbohydrate Choice: 2

 **Snow White's Tip:** Cooking for seven can be tricky, but this recipe makes it simple! Little members of the household can have fun measuring out all the ingredients, stirring the mixture, and pouring it onto the cookie sheet.

9

Goofy's Tip: You can't make a frittata without breaking a few eggs! Young ones can practice their egg-cracking skills and then stir the mixture—just don't let them get whisked away.

Goofy's
Zucchini Frittata

Serving: ⅛ slice
Calories: 125
Total Fat: 9g
Total Carbohydrate: 3g
Fiber: 1g
Protein: 9g
Carbohydrate Choice: 0

Gluten-free

Ingredients

2 to 3 small zucchini
6 eggs
8 to 10 large basil leaves, chopped or torn
2 tablespoons chopped fresh parsley
¾ cup freshly grated Parmesan

Salt and pepper
3 slices bacon
1 small, ripe tomato, seeded and diced
4 scallions, chopped
1 tablespoon butter

Instructions

1. Coarsely grate enough of the zucchini to make 2 ½ cups and place it in a medium-size mixing bowl. Lightly salt the zucchini and toss it gently to season it evenly. Let it sit for 10 minutes, then use clean hands to squeeze the zucchini, pressing out the excess water.
2. In a large mixing bowl, whisk the eggs until they are evenly blended. Whisk in the basil, parsley, about half of the Parmesan, ¼ teaspoon salt, and ⅛ teaspoon pepper. Set the mixture aside.
3. Heat a 10-inch ovenproof nonstick skillet on the stove top. Add the bacon and cook it over medium heat until it is crisp, about 6 to 8 minutes. Transfer the bacon to a paper towel-lined plate. Spoon all but 1 tablespoon of the bacon fat out of the pan. Heat the broiler.
4. Add the grated zucchini to the skillet and sauté it over high heat for 3 minutes, stirring occasionally. While the zucchini is cooking, chop or crumble the bacon into small pieces and add it to the egg mixture.
5. Add the diced tomato and scallions to the skillet and sauté the vegetables until they are soft but not mushy, about 2 to 3 minutes. Add the butter to the skillet in pieces and stir it into the vegetables. Use a fork to loosely arrange the vegetables in an even layer in the pan.
6. Whisk the egg mixture again, then slowly pour it over the vegetables, covering the entire surface. Do not stir the mixture. Instead, gently shake the pan to help settle the egg. Cook the frittata over medium heat for 4 minutes without disturbing it.
7. Sprinkle the remaining cheese evenly over the top of the frittata. Place the pan under the broiler about 8 inches from the heat source and broil the frittata for about 2 minutes.
8. Using an oven mitt, remove the pan from the oven and poke a fork in the center of the frittata to see if it's done. If you see liquid egg around the fork, place the pan back under the broiler for another 45 to 60 seconds. When the frittata is done, transfer the pan to a cooling rack.
9. Let the frittata cool in the pan for 5 minutes, then carefully slide a flexible spatula around the edge to loosen it. Once it's free, gently lift the frittata with the spatula, tilt the pan, and slide it onto a large serving plate. Let it cool at least 5 more minutes, then slice it into wedges and serve.

Piglet's Tip: P-p-p-pancakes are p-p-p-pretty great! Kids can tag team on this project—one can mix the eggs and oil while the other mixes the dry ingredients.

Piglet's
Oatmeal Pancakes

Ingredients

2 eggs
2 tablespoons vegetable oil
1 cup all-purpose flour, or ½ cup all-purpose
   and ½ cup whole wheat
1 cup rolled oats

1½ teaspoons baking powder
½ teaspoon salt
¾ cup orange juice (preferably fresh)
2 tablespoons butter

Instructions

1. In a small bowl, mix the eggs with the oil. In a medium-size bowl, combine the dry ingredients.
2. Stir the egg mixture into the dry ingredients, then stir in enough orange juice to create a thick batter.
3. Heat the butter in a large frying pan, then pour batter into the pan by quarter cupfuls. Cook until done, turning once.

Serving: 2 pancakes
Calories: 322
Total Fat: 16g
Total Carbohydrate: 37g
Fiber: 3g
Protein: 8g
Carbohydrate Choice: 2 ½

Hercules's
Oven Eggs with Ham

Ingredients

1 medium onion, finely chopped (about 1 ½ cups)
1 teaspoon butter
1 teaspoon olive oil
4 medium leaves Swiss chard, stems removed and leaves finely chopped (about 1 cup)
6 whole eggs

6 egg whites
1 cup light sour cream
⅓ cup chopped fresh Italian parsley
1 ½ cups cooked, diced ham (about 7 ounces)
2 ½ cups grated reduced-fat Swiss or sharp cheddar

Instructions

1. In a medium-size skillet, sauté the onion in the butter and olive oil until soft and translucent, about 5 minutes. Add the chard and cook until just wilted, about 1 minute. Let cool.
2. In a bowl, beat together the eggs and egg whites. Stir in the sour cream, parsley, ham, chard mixture, and 2 cups of the cheese.
3. Pour the mixture into a greased 9x13-inch glass baking dish. Cover it with plastic wrap and refrigerate overnight, or bake it (uncovered) immediately.
4. Heat the oven to 375°F. If the casserole was refrigerated overnight, let it sit for 15 minutes at room temperature. Bake until it has set, about 35 to 40 minutes.
5. Sprinkle the casserole with the remaining cheese and bake until the cheese melts, about 3 minutes.

Serving: ¹⁄₁₂ piece
Calories: 150
Total Fat: 7g
Total Carbohydrate: 4g
Fiber: 0g
Protein: 16g
Carbohydrate Choice: 0

Gluten-free

 **Hercules's Tip:** The protein in this breakfast is just what every hero-in-training needs! Parents should take charge when using the range, but the younger set can still scoop out the sour cream and even try separating the eggs.

Cinderella's Tip: This coffee cake is as easy as saying *bibbidi bobbidi boo*! Little chefs can measure out and mix the dry ingredients, sprinkle on the topping, and marbleize the batter.

Cinderella's
Dream-Come-True Coffee Cake

Ingredients

COFFEE CAKE
2 cups all-purpose flour
1 teaspoon baking powder
½ teaspoon baking soda
½ teaspoon salt
¼ cup sugar
1 tablespoon melted butter
1 egg, at room temperature
1 ½ cups buttermilk, at room temperature

TOPPING
⅓ cup brown sugar
½ cup chopped nuts (pecans or walnuts)
2 teaspoons cinnamon

Instructions

1. Heat the oven to 375°F. Grease a 9-inch-round cake pan with 2-inch sides.
2. In a large mixing bowl, combine all the dry ingredients.
3. In a medium-size bowl, combine the butter, egg, and buttermilk. Add the buttermilk mixture to the dry ingredients and stir until combined. Pour the batter into the prepared pan.
4. Mix together all the topping ingredients and sprinkle evenly over the batter. Run a knife or spoon through the pan, allowing the topping to invade the batter. You don't want to mix the two; you're aiming for a marbled effect.
5. Bake for 25 to 30 minutes or until a toothpick comes out clean. Serve warm.

Serving: ⅛ piece
Calories: 249
Total Fat: 7g
Total Carbohydrate: 38g
Fiber: 2g
Protein: 7g
Carbohydrate Choice: 2 ½

Mrs. Potts's
Maple French Toast

Ingredients

4 eggs, beaten
½ cup low-fat milk
1 teaspoon vanilla extract
2 tablespoons oil
8 slices dense bread
3 ounces grated maple sugar candy

Instructions

1. Mix the eggs, milk, and vanilla extract in a shallow bowl or pie plate.
2. Heat the oil in a heavy-bottomed skillet over medium heat.
3. Soak the slices of bread in the egg mixture, turning once. They should be saturated but not falling apart.
4. Brown the bread in the skillet, turning once, about 2 to 3 minutes on each side. Then sprinkle grated maple sugar candy on the top and turn. Cook for 1 minute.
5. Sprinkle the other side with maple sugar and turn once more. Now both sides of the toast should have a crisp, sugary coating.
6. Add butter to the pan between each batch. Allow the toast to cool for a minute before serving.

Serving: 1 slice
Calories: 213
Total Fat: 9g
Total Carbohydrate: 26g
Fiber: 3g
Protein: 7g
Carbohydrate Choice: 2

Gluten-free note: prepare with gluten-free bread (carbohydrate amount will vary).

Mrs. Potts's Tip: Why not serve this French toast with a nice pot of tea? While Mom or Dad handles the skillet, kids can dip the bread in the egg mixture and sprinkle on the maple candy.

Aurora's Tip: Muffins this yummy are worth waking up for! As long as Mom or Dad uses the oven, junior cooks can help with every step in this recipe.

Aurora's
Applesauce Muffins

Ingredients

6 tablespoons butter
1 ½ cups all-purpose flour
1 teaspoon baking powder
½ teaspoon baking soda
1 teaspoon cinnamon

½ teaspoon salt
2 eggs
⅔ cup brown sugar
1 ½ cups chunky applesauce

Instructions

1. Heat the oven to 375°F. Line a 12-cup muffin tin with baking cups and set aside. In a small microwave-safe bowl, melt the butter on high for about 30 to 60 seconds; set aside to cool slightly.
2. Sift together the flour, baking powder, baking soda, cinnamon, and salt into a large mixing bowl.
3. In another bowl, whisk together the eggs and brown sugar. Stir in the applesauce and melted butter until the mixture is smooth.
4. Pour the apple mixture over the flour mixture. Mix with a wooden spoon until combined (it's ready when you can't see any traces of flour).
5. Fill the baking cups about two-thirds full with batter. Bake for 20 minutes or until lightly brown.

Serving: 1 muffin
Calories: 176
Total Fat: 7g
Total Carbohydrate: 25
Fiber: 1g
Protein: 3g
Carbohydrate Choice: 1 ½

Peter Pan's
Pumpkin Waffles

Ingredients

2 cups all-purpose flour
¼ cup sugar
1 tablespoon baking powder
1 teaspoon cinnamon
½ teaspoon salt

2 eggs
1 ½ cups skim milk
4 tablespoons butter, melted
½ cup canned pumpkin

Instructions

1. Set up the waffle iron on a countertop or table within easy reach. Plug in the iron to preheat it.
2. In a medium-size mixing bowl, stir together the flour, sugar, baking powder, cinnamon, and salt. In a separate mixing bowl, whisk together the eggs, milk, melted butter, and pumpkin. Pour the wet ingredients over the flour mixture and stir just until combined.
3. Coat the preheated waffle iron with cooking spray. Pour the waffle batter onto the center of each section of the iron. (You will need ¼ to ¾ cup of batter for each waffle.)
4. Cook the waffles for about 4 to 5 minutes or until they are crispy and light brown. (Read the manufacturer's directions for details about how long you should cook the waffles in your particular waffle iron.) Serve immediately with maple syrup and butter.

Serving: ⅔ cup batter or
   2, 4-inch-square waffles
   (does not include syrup
   and additional butter)
Calories: 308
Total Fat: 10g
Total Carbohydrate: 44g
Fiber: 2g
Protein: 9g
Carbohydrate Choice: 3

Flour

Peter's Tip: You won't need any pixie dust to make these tasty waffles—just a bit of cinnamon! Kids can almost fly on their own, from measuring the ingredients to mixing the batter. But only grown-ups should use the waffle iron.

LUNCH

Baloo's Tip: Papa bear loves his chili—especially when it has a kick! Cubs can pitch in by measuring the spices and grating the cheese.

Serving: 1 cup (does not include garnishes)
Calories: 271
Total Fat: 9g
Total Carbohydrate: 23g
Fiber: 9g
Protein: 18g
Carbohydrate Choice: 1

Gluten-free note: prepare with gluten-free chicken broth.

Baloo's
Beef and Black Bean Chili

Ingredients

CHILI
Southwest Seasoning Mix (see next column)
½ pound ground beef
Vegetable oil
1 large onion, chopped
1 medium green bell pepper, chopped
1 clove garlic, minced
1 ½ cups tomato juice
1 ½ to 2 cups beef or chicken stock
1 cup canned crushed tomatoes in puree
3 to 4 cups cooked black or red beans
¾ teaspoon salt
Black pepper, to taste
Sour cream, grated cheddar cheese, and/or
   chopped parsley, for garnish

SOUTHWEST SEASONING MIX
1 tablespoon cumin
1 tablespoon mild chili powder
1 ½ teaspoons coriander
1 teaspoon dried oregano
1 teaspoon unsweetened cocoa powder

Instructions

1. In a small bowl, blend all of the ingredients for the Southwest Seasoning Mix, then set the bowl aside.
2. Heat a medium-size casserole or Dutch oven. Add the ground beef and brown over medium heat for several minutes. Using a slotted spoon, transfer the meat to a small bowl and set it aside.
3. If there's very little fat left in the pan, add 1 to 2 tablespoons of vegetable oil. Add the onion and green pepper and sauté over moderate heat for 8 to 9 minutes, until the onion is translucent. Add the garlic and seasoning mix, stirring constantly for 30 seconds.
4. Stir in the remaining ingredients and the reserved meat, using enough stock to achieve a consistency that is neither too thin nor too thick. Bring the mixture to a simmer gently for 10 to 15 minutes, stirring often. Thin the chili with a little more stock if necessary. Serve hot with the garnishes.

Dumbo's
Corn Chowder

Ingredients

2 tablespoons butter
½ cup finely chopped green onion
¾ cup diced red bell pepper
¾ cup chopped celery
1 pound potatoes (about 3 medium), peeled and
  diced into ½-inch-thick pieces

4 cups fresh corn kernels (from about 8 ears)
1 bay leaf
4 cups low-sodium chicken broth
2 cups whole milk
Salt and pepper
Sour cream for garnish (optional)

Instructions

1. In a large saucepan, melt the butter over medium-low heat. Add the green onions, bell pepper, and celery, and cook, stirring occasionally, until the vegetables start to soften, about 10 minutes. Stir in the potatoes, 2 cups of the corn, the bay leaf, and the broth.
2. Bring the mixture to a boil, then reduce the heat and keep it at a simmer for 15 minutes, stirring occasionally.
3. Puree the remaining 2 cups of corn and the milk in a blender or food processor, then stir it into the soup. Simmer the soup until it thickens slightly, 5 to 10 minutes. Remove the bay leaf and add salt and pepper to taste. Top each serving with a dollop of sour cream, if desired.

Serving: 1 ½ cups (does not
  include garnishes)
Calories: 254
Total Fat: 7g
Total Carbohydrate: 36g
Fiber: 5g
Protein: 12g
Carbohydrate Choice: 2

Gluten-free note: prepare with
gluten-free chicken broth.

Dumbo's Tip: Chowder this tasty will give you ears—er, wings—to fly! While Mom or Dad chops the peppers and onions, young ones can husk the corn. To remove all that pesky silk, huskers should hold the ear in one hand and rub downward with a wet paper towel.

29

Jasmine's Tip: A whole new world of flavor awaits with this chunky stew! Little ones can drain the tomatoes and measure out the chicken stock and flour, while big kids chop the veggies. To cut an onion without crying, try breathing through your mouth or putting on a pair of swim goggles!

Jasmine's
Mulligatawny

Ingredients

4 tablespoons butter (or 2 tablespoons olive oil)
1 onion, chopped
2 carrots, chopped
1 celery stalk, chopped
1 green pepper, chopped
1 apple, cored, peeled, and chopped
1 ½ pounds raw boneless, skinless chicken breast, chopped

½ cup flour
2 to 3 teaspoons curry powder
5 cups chicken broth
1 (14 ½-ounce) can diced tomatoes, drained
Salt and pepper
2 cups hot cooked rice

Instructions

1. Melt the butter, or heat the oil, in a large pot over medium heat. Add the onion, carrots, celery, green pepper, apple, and chicken, and sauté for about 15 minutes. Turn the heat to low.
2. In a small bowl, mix together the flour and curry powder. Add the mixture to the pot, then stir and cook for 3 to 5 minutes. Add the chicken broth and tomatoes. Partially cover the pot and simmer the soup for about an hour, stirring occasionally. Add the salt and pepper to taste.
3. To serve, place ¼ cup of rice in a bowl and ladle the soup over the rice.

Serving: ¼ cup rice with
   1 cup soup
Calories: 295
Total Fat: 9g
Total Carbohydrate: 24g
Fiber: 2g
Protein: 27g
Carbohydrate Choice: 1 ½

Rapunzel's
Chicken and Biscuit Pie

Ingredients

FILLING
4 tablespoons butter
1 cup finely chopped onion
1 rib celery, finely chopped
⅓ cup flour
1 ½ cups chicken stock
1 ½ cups whole milk
½ teaspoon dried sage
½ teaspoon dried thyme
2 ½ cups diced cooked chicken
2 cups vegetables of your choice (leftovers or frozen ones that have been thawed)
Salt and pepper

BISCUIT TOPPING
2 cups flour
1 tablespoon baking powder
1 teaspoon sugar
½ teaspoon salt
¼ cup cold unsalted butter, cut into ¼-inch pieces
¾ cup reduced fat (2%) milk

Instructions

1. Melt the butter on the stove top in a Dutch oven or other oven-safe sauté pan with high sides. Stir in the onion and celery, then cover the pan and cook them for 7 to 8 minutes over medium heat, stirring occasionally. Add the flour, stirring for 1 to 2 minutes to lightly brown it.

2. Whisk the chicken stock into the pan. When it starts to thicken, whisk in the milk. Add the sage, thyme, chicken, and vegetables, continuing to stir until the mixture is heated through, about 5 to 7 minutes. Add salt and pepper to taste.

3. Remove the pan from the stove top and heat the oven to 375°F. Meanwhile, make the biscuit topping by combining the flour, baking powder, sugar, and salt in a mixing bowl. Add the butter and use your fingertips to rub it into the dry ingredients. Add the milk and stir briskly, just until the dough pulls together.

4. Flour your work surface and turn the dough onto it. Using floured hands, knead the dough two or three times, then flatten it to about ½-inch thick. Using a small round cutter, cut the dough into 24 biscuits and place as many as will fit, barely touching, on top of the filling. (You can bake any extras separately on a lightly greased pie plate, for about 15 minutes.)

5. Bake the potpie until the biscuits are golden brown and the filling is bubbly, about 20 to 30 minutes. Then let it cool for 5 to 10 minutes before serving it.

Serving: 3 biscuits and 1 cup of filling
Calories: 366
Total Fat: 16g
Total Carbohydrate: 35g
Fiber: 2g
Protein: 19g
Carbohydrate Choice: 2

Rapunzel's Tip: The way I see it, cooking is a really good excuse to get your hands dirty! Kids will love working the butter into the biscuit dough.

Alice's
Chicken Salad Tea Sandwiches

Ingredients

1 ½ pounds raw boneless, skinless chicken breasts
1 small onion, quartered
1 ½ teaspoons tarragon
½ to ¾ cup mayonnaise
20 green grapes
Salt and pepper, to taste
⅓ cup slivered almonds (optional)
16 slices bread of choice

Instructions

1. To make the salad, cut the chicken into 2-inch cubes and place in a saucepan. (Thoroughly wash your hands and the cutting board afterward.)
2. Add water to cover, mix in the onion and 1 teaspoon of the tarragon, and cook over high heat.
3. Once the water boils, reduce the heat and simmer for 20 minutes. For best results, check the chicken for doneness: the center should be white with no traces of pink.
4. Drain the water from the saucepan and transfer the chicken to a cutting board. Remove the onion, but don't remove the tarragon.
5. Cut the chicken into small pieces and place it in a large bowl.
6. Add the mayonnaise and toss well.
7. Slice the grapes and add them to the bowl, then stir in salt, pepper, and additional tarragon to taste. Stir in the almonds, if desired. Cover the salad and refrigerate.
8. To assemble a tea sandwich, remove the crusts from 2 slices of bread, add the chicken salad filling, and cut the resulting sandwich into squares or triangles. Makes about 3 cups chicken salad, enough for 8 full-size sandwiches.

Serving: 1 full-size sandwich, or 4 tea sandwiches
Calories: 429
Total Fat: 18g
Total Carbohydrate: 40g
Fiber: 3g
Protein: 26g
Carbohydrate Choice: 2 ½**

Gluten-free note: serve with gluten-free bread or wrap (carbohydrate amount will vary).

**Chicken salad alone contains 4g total carbohydrate per ⅓ cup serving.

 **Alice's Tip:** No tea party—or *unbirthday* party—is complete without these sandwiches! For safety's sake, ask kids to use a plastic knife instead of a sharp one to cut the grapes.

Sebastian's
Smoky Rice and Beans

Ingredients

1 tablespoon olive oil
½ cup diced onion
½ teaspoon ground cumin
1 teaspoon minced canned chipotle pepper
1 cup white rice
1 cup canned black beans, drained and rinsed

½ cup canned diced tomatoes, drained
½ cup frozen corn (optional)
Salt and pepper, to taste
2 cups chicken broth
2 tablespoons chopped scallion greens (optional)

Instructions

1. Heat the oil in a medium-size saucepan over medium heat. Add the onion, cumin, and chipotle pepper. Cook for 5 minutes, stirring occasionally, or until the onion starts to soften.

2. Add the rice and stir to coat with the oil. Add the black beans, tomatoes, and corn. Season with salt and pepper. Add the chicken broth and bring to a boil. Reduce the heat to low, cover, and simmer for about 25 minutes, or until all the liquid is absorbed.

3. Remove from the heat and let stand for 10 minutes. Transfer to a serving bowl, then sprinkle with scallions, if desired.

Serving: about 1 cup
Calories: 207
Total Fat: 3g
Total Carbohydrate: 36g
Fiber: 3g
Protein: 8g
Carbohydrate Choice: 2 ½

Gluten-free note: prepare with gluten-free chicken broth.

Sebastian's Tip: Rice and beans together are like music to my ears! Wee crustaceans can join in the symphony by rinsing and draining the canned beans and tomatoes, and measuring the rice and frozen corn.

Tigger's
Tortellini Vegetable Soup

Ingredients

2 tablespoons olive oil
1 medium onion, chopped
1 small zucchini, diced
1 medium carrot, peeled and diced
5 ½ cups chicken stock
1 teaspoon dried basil (more if fresh)

1 bay leaf
½ cup canned crushed tomatoes
½ teaspoon salt
9 ounces fresh or frozen tortellini (cheese or meat filled)
2 to 3 tablespoons chopped fresh parsley
Black pepper, to taste

Instructions

1. Heat the olive oil in a medium soup pot or large saucepan. Add the onion, zucchini, and carrot. Sauté over moderate heat for 8 to 10 minutes, stirring often, until the onion is soft and translucent.
2. Add the stock, basil, bay leaf, tomatoes, and salt to the pot. Increase the heat and bring the mixture to a low boil. Add the tortellini and bring the soup back to a low boil. Cook it for 2 minutes, then reduce the heat and let it simmer for 5 to 6 minutes longer. Gently stir in the parsley and pepper during the last minute or so.

Serving: about 1 ½ cups
Calories: 177
Total Fat: 7g
Total Carbohydrate: 15g
Fiber: 2g
Protein: 13g
Carbohydrate Choice: 1

Gluten-free note: substitute gluten-free pasta (carbohydrate amount will vary).

Tigger's Tip: Peeling carrots is something that Tiggers—and kids—do best!

Tiana's Tip: Nothing brings folks together like good gumbo! Only grown-ups should use the grill, but big kids can chop the veggies while little kids set the table.

Serving: 1½ cups
  (does not include rice)
Calories: 276
Total Fat: 14g
Total Carbohydrate: 9g
Fiber: 3g
Protein: 27g
Carbohydrate Choice: ½

Gluten-free note: prepare with gluten-free ketchup; check ingredients in sausage and seasoning mix.

Tiana's
Grilled Shrimp Gumbo

Ingredients

1 pound large shrimp, peeled and deveined
12 ounces andouille sausage, halved lengthwise
1 pint grape tomatoes
¾ pound finger-size okra, stems trimmed
1 onion, sliced into ¼-inch-thick rings
1 red bell pepper, cored, seeded, and cut into
  8 pieces
1 green bell pepper, cored, seeded, and cut into
  8 pieces

¼ cup olive oil
2 teaspoons Creole or Cajun seasoning
2 tablespoons ketchup
4 green onions, chopped
Coarse salt and pepper, to taste
Cooked rice

Instructions

1. Place the shrimp, sausage, tomatoes, okra, onion, and peppers in a large bowl. Add the oil and Creole or Cajun seasoning, and toss to coat the ingredients. Thread the shrimp, tomatoes, okra, and onion onto separate skewers. Shortcut: use a grilling basket instead of skewers for the vegetables.

2. Prepare the grill for cooking. If using a gas grill, start it on high, then reduce the temperature to medium-high as soon as the grill is heated.

3. Place the vegetables on the hottest part of the grill. Arrange the sausage over slightly cooler heat and the shrimp at the edges of the grill. Cook, turning once or twice, until the shrimp is opaque, the sausage is cooked through, and the vegetables are tender and slightly charred, about 8 to 10 minutes (shrimp may take less time to cook). Slice the sausage, onion, and bell peppers into bite-size pieces, then transfer them, along with the other ingredients, to a large bowl.

4. Toss the meat and vegetable mixture with the ketchup and green onions. Cover the mixture tightly with plastic wrap and let the vegetables steam and wilt slightly, about 3 to 5 minutes.

5. Remove the plastic wrap from the bowl. Taste and adjust the seasoning with salt, pepper, and Creole or Cajun seasoning to your liking. Serve over cooked rice.

Genie's
Guacamole Potato Salad

Ingredients

3 pounds red potatoes
2 tablespoons, plus 1 to 1 ½ teaspoons salt
1 ripe avocado, peeled
2 teaspoons grated lime zest
Juice of 2 limes (about ½ cup)

2 garlic cloves, crushed
½ cup chopped cilantro
2 tablespoons light mayonnaise
2 celery stalks, sliced

Instructions

1. In a large pot, cover the potatoes with cold water. Add the 2 tablespoons of salt and bring the potatoes to a boil over high heat. Reduce the heat to medium and simmer until the potatoes are tender, about 20 minutes, or until you can pierce them easily with a paring knife. Drain them in a colander and allow to cool.

2. Meanwhile, puree the avocado, lime zest and juice, garlic, cilantro, mayonnaise, and remaining salt in a food processor until smooth. If the dressing seems too thick, add a tablespoon or so of hot water.

3. Cut the potatoes into bite-size chunks (leave the skins on) and place them in a large bowl with the celery. Scrape in the dressing with a rubber spatula and gently stir it all together. Serve immediately, or cover and chill.

Serving: about 1 cup
Calories: 184
Total Fat: 5g
Total Carbohydrate: 30g
Fiber: 4g
Protein: 4g
Carbohydrate Choice: 1 ½

Gluten-free note: prepare with gluten-free mayonnaise.

Genie's Tip: This potato salad is as good as a magic carpet ride through the Cave of Wonders! Mom or Dad should handle the food processor, but little chefs can juice and zest the limes.

Captain Hook's
Cape Codder Sandwich

Ingredients

3 slices low-sodium turkey, roasted or store-bought
2 tablespoons cranberry sauce
¼ cup stuffing

Lettuce, shredded
1 slice red onion
2 slices marbled rye or pumpernickel bread

Instructions

1. Spread the cranberry sauce on one slice of bread. Stack with turkey, stuffing, lettuce, and onion. Top with remaining slice of bread.

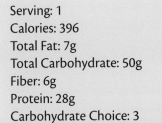

Serving: 1
Calories: 396
Total Fat: 7g
Total Carbohydrate: 50g
Fiber: 6g
Protein: 28g
Carbohydrate Choice: 3

Gluten-free note: prepare with gluten-free stuffing and serve with gluten-free bread or wrap (carbohydrate amount will vary).

Captain Hook's Tip: If I can make this sandwich with one hand and one hook, any young landlubber can do it!

DINNER

Mushu's
Asian Pulled-Pork Sandwiches

Ingredients

½ cup low-sodium soy sauce
½ cup hoisin sauce
3 tablespoons ketchup
3 tablespoons rice vinegar
¼ cup honey
3 cloves garlic, minced
1 ½ tablespoons peeled and grated fresh ginger

2 teaspoons dark sesame oil
1 ½ teaspoons Chinese five-spice powder
4 pounds boneless Boston butt pork roast, trimmed of fat and cut into 2-inch chunks (you can substitute beef brisket)
10 buns

Instructions

1. Add everything but the meat and buns to the slow cooker and whisk to combine. Add the pork and toss it to coat. Cover and cook the meat on low for 8 hours.

2. When the pork is done, remove it from the slow cooker with a slotted spoon and place it on a cutting board. Shred the pork by pulling the pieces apart with two forks.

3. Return the meat to the cooker, stir it into the remaining sauce, and then serve it on the buns. If you like, make the dish up to 2 days ahead and store it covered in the refrigerator.

4. Simply skim off any accumulated fat and reheat the meat in a saucepan over low heat before serving.

Serving: about 1 sandwich
Calories: 508
Total Fat: 21g
Total Carbohydrate: 36g
Fiber: 2g
Protein: 42g
Carbohydrate Choice: 2 ½

Gluten-free note: prepare with gluten-free soy sauce, hoisin sauce, and ketchup; serve with gluten-free bun/bread, corn tortilla, or rice (carbohydrate amount will vary).

Mushu's Tip: Guard this recipe with your life; your family will enjoy it for generations to come! The best part about making these sandwiches is shredding the pork—and little hands can do that just as easily as big ones!

Simba's Tip: Making steak stir-fry is roaring good fun! Cubs can lend a paw by measuring out all the ingredients, from the salt and cornstarch to the vinegar and beef broth.

Serving: 1 ¾ cups
  (does not include rice or
  optional ingredients)
Calories: 258
Total Fat: 14g
Total Carbohydrate: 3g Fiber:
1g
Protein: 28g
Carbohydrate Choice: 0

Gluten-free note: prepare
with gluten-free soy sauce,
hoisin sauce, and beef broth.

Simba's
Steak Stir-Fry

Ingredients

1 ½ pounds boneless shell sirloin steak, trimmed and sliced thin (2-inch-long x ½-inch-wide strips)
1 egg white
1 teaspoon salt
1 tablespoon lite soy sauce
2 teaspoons cornstarch
1 tablespoon hoisin sauce
1 tablespoon rice vinegar
⅓ cup canned low-salt fat-free beef broth

½ teaspoon cornstarch mixed with ½ teaspoon water
1 teaspoon sesame oil
1 tablespoon peanut oil
2 teaspoons peeled and finely chopped fresh ginger
8 ounces pea pods, trimmed
1 medium red bell pepper, cut into ¼-inch strips
½ cup unsalted roasted peanuts (optional)
1 tablespoon red pepper flakes (optional)

Instructions

1. Whisk the egg white in a medium-size bowl until foamy, then whisk in the salt and cornstarch. Stir in the beef and set aside.
2. In a separate bowl, mix the soy, hoisin, vinegar, broth, cornstarch-water mixture, and sesame oil; set the sauce aside.
3. In a wok, heat the peanut oil on high. Add the beef and stir-fry until lightly browned. Add the ginger and stir-fry 30 seconds. Add the sauce, pea pods, and bell pepper and stir-fry for 1 to 3 minutes.
4. Finish by adding the optional peanuts and red pepper flakes.

Mowgli's
Moroccan Chicken Kebobs

Ingredients

DRY RUB
1 teaspoon cinnamon
½ teaspoon salt
½ teaspoon cumin
½ teaspoon turmeric
¼ teaspoon cayenne (optional)
¼ teaspoon pepper
¼ teaspoon cardamom
⅛ teaspoon ground cloves
⅛ teaspoon nutmeg
2 teaspoons brown sugar

KEBOBS
2 pounds boneless, skinless chicken breasts
2 small red onions, peeled and cut into
    1-inch-wide sections
2 bell peppers, cleaned and cut into 1-inch
    squares
¼ cup olive oil
Salt and pepper, to taste
12 (10-inch) bamboo skewers, soaked in
    water for 30 minutes

Instructions

1. In a small bowl, combine the dry rub ingredients and mix well.
2. Cut the meat into 1 ½-inch cubes and put them in a gallon-size resealable plastic bag with the rub mix. Seal the bag and shake it vigorously until all the chicken is well coated.
3. Place the onions and peppers in a gallon-size resealable plastic bag, add the olive oil, and season with salt and pepper. Seal the bag and shake it vigorously to coat the vegetables well.
4. Assemble the kebobs by alternately skewering pieces of chicken, onions, and peppers.
5. Prepare a charcoal fire, or set a gas grill to medium-high, close the lid, and heat until hot, about 10 to 15 minutes.
6. Grill the kebobs, turning occasionally, until the chicken is no longer pink inside, about 8 to 10 minutes on a gas grill.

Serving: 2 skewers
Calories: 287
Total Fat: 13g
Total Carbohydrate: 4g
Fiber: 1g
Protein: 35g
Carbohydrate Choice: 0

Gluten-free

Mowgli's Tip: If you've got a loving family and yummy food to make with them, you've got the bare necessities! Small fries will love measuring all the spices and shaking them up with the chicken.

Ariel's
Turkey Pilaf

Ingredients

1 onion
3 carrots
2 cups fresh spinach (3 handfuls)
1 ¼ pounds lean ground turkey
2 ½ cups water
6-ounce package rice pilaf mix

2 tablespoons margarine
1 cup raisins
¾ cup pine nuts

Instructions

1. Peel and chop the onion and carrots. Rinse the spinach, remove the stems, and tear it into bite-size pieces.
2. In a saucepan over medium-high heat, brown the turkey, stirring to break up the meat, for about 5 minutes, or until it begins to brown.
3. Pour off any liquid. Add the chopped onion and carrots and cook for 3 more minutes.
4. Add the water, rice mix, and butter or margarine, and stir well. Add the raisins, pine nuts, and spinach.
5. Cover and simmer over low heat, stirring occasionally, for 25 minutes.

Serving: about 1 cup
Calories: 370
Total Fat: 18g
Total Carbohydrate: 35g
Fiber: 3g
Protein: 20g
Carbohydrate Choice: 2

Gluten-free note: prepare with gluten-free rice pilaf mix (carbohydrate amount may vary).

Ariel's Tip: So this is what you really use a dinglehopper for! While Mom or Dad cooks the turkey, guppies can tear the spinach and measure out the raisins and pine nuts.

Prince Phillip's
Baked Potato Wedges

Ingredients

2 tablespoons canola oil
1 cup flour
1 teaspoon garlic powder
1 teaspoon salt
1 teaspoon black pepper

½ teaspoon celery salt
½ teaspoon seasoning salt
2 large eggs
4 medium potatoes (1 ⅓ pound), scrubbed and rinsed but not peeled
Canola cooking spray

Instructions

1. Heat the oven to 450°F. Coat a baking sheet with a tablespoon of canola oil.
2. With a fork or whisk, mix the flour, garlic powder, salt, pepper, celery salt, and seasoning salt in a shallow dish and set aside. Crack the eggs into a small bowl and beat with a fork.
3. Cut each potato into 16 half-inch-thick wedges. Dip each wedge into the beaten eggs, then the flour mixture, making sure it is well coated. Place the coated wedges on the prepared baking sheet and let them sit 10 to 15 minutes.
4. Coat the tops of the potato wedges generously with canola cooking spray. Bake in the center of the oven until golden brown (15 to 18 minutes), flipping after 10 minutes.

Serving: about 12 wedges
    (6 ounces)
Calories: 261
Total Fat: 8g
Total Carbohydrate: 39g
Fiber: 3g
Protein: 8g
Carbohydrate Choice: 2 ½

Prince Phillip's Tip: These potatoes are a great part of a hearty meal, perfect after a long day of riding and dragon slaying. Young heroes will have fun dipping the potato wedges in the egg and flour mixture.

Mulan's Tip: Girl or boy, warrior or farmer, everyone likes egg fried rice! Little chefs in training can crack and beat the eggs and then practice their chopstick moves while Mom or Dad cooks the rice.

Serving: 1 cup
Calories: 248
Total Fat: 9g
Total Carbohydrate: 33g
Fiber: 3g
Protein: 8g
Carbohydrate Choice: 2

Gluten-free note: prepare with gluten-free soy sauce.

Mulan's
Egg Fried Rice

Ingredients

2 ½ tablespoons vegetable oil
½ teaspoon sesame oil
4 scallions, sliced
1 cup frozen baby peas, thawed

1 medium carrot, peeled and grated
3 cups cooked and chilled long-grain white rice
3 large eggs
1 ½ to 2 tablespoons lite soy sauce

Instructions

1. Heat 2 tablespoons of the vegetable oil and the sesame oil in a large sauté pan or wok over medium heat. Add the scallions, peas, and grated carrot all at once, taking care to avoid being splattered by hot oil. Sauté the vegetables for 1 minute, stirring them constantly. Add the rice and stir the mixture occasionally as it heats for 2 to 3 minutes.
2. Break the eggs into a small bowl and beat them with a fork or small whisk until blended. Then move the rice to the perimeter of the pan and pour the remaining ½ tablespoon of vegetable oil into the center. Add the eggs and stir them continuously with a wooden spoon until they are soft but not overcooked.
3. When the eggs are almost fully cooked, stir the rice into them until everything is well mixed. Add the soy sauce and heat for another minute or two, stirring often.

Stitch's
Chicken Teriyaki

Ingredients

MARINADE
¼ cup ketchup
¼ cup hoisin sauce
2 tablespoons soy sauce
2 tablespoons rice vinegar
2 teaspoons minced fresh garlic
2 teaspoons minced fresh ginger
2 teaspoons dark sesame oil

CHICKEN TERIYAKI
8 boneless, skinless chicken thighs (about 4 ounces each)
Sesame seeds, toasted in a skillet
Scallion tops, cut into 2-inch-long strips (optional)

Instructions

1. Place the chicken thighs in a gallon-size resealable plastic bag and add the marinade ingredients. Press the air out of the bag and seal it. Turn the bag to thoroughly coat the chicken, then place it in a bowl and refrigerate it for at least 4 hours (preferably overnight), turning the bag occasionally. Remove the meat from the refrigerator 20 minutes before grilling.

2. Prepare a charcoal fire or set a gas grill to medium-high, close the lid, and heat until hot—about 10 to 15 minutes.

3. Remove the chicken from the bag and discard the marinade. Grill the thighs until they are no longer pink inside, about 5 minutes per side on a gas grill.

4. Transfer the thighs to a cutting board and let them rest for about 5 minutes, then slice each piece at a diagonal. Sprinkle on the toasted sesame seeds. Serve over rice, garnished, if you like, with scallion strips.

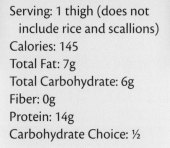

Serving: 1 thigh (does not
   include rice and scallions)
Calories: 145
Total Fat: 7g
Total Carbohydrate: 6g
Fiber: 0g
Protein: 14g
Carbohydrate Choice: ½

Gluten-free note: prepare
using gluten-free ketchup,
hoisin sauce, vinegar, and
soy sauce.

Stitch's Tip: *Ohana* means family, and family means you always have someone to cook with! Only parents should use the grill, but kids can measure out the marinade ingredients and sprinkle on the sesame seeds.

Cogsworth's Tip: This dinner will satisfy even the most beastly appetite! While Mom and Dad cut the potatoes, kids can bang away at the melba toast with kitchen mallets.

Serving: 6 ounces of fish,
  8 potato wedges
  (4 ounces)
Calories: 410
Total Fat: 12g
Total Carbohydrate: 45g
Fiber: 3g
Protein: 31g
Carbohydrate Choice: 3

Cogsworth's
Oven-Fried Fish and Chips

Ingredients

4 all-purpose baking potatoes (1 ⅓ pound),
  such as russet or Idaho
2 tablespoons olive oil
1 teaspoon paprika
Salt and pepper, to taste
1 box melba toast, Mediterranean or garlic
  flavored (about 5 ounces)

2 large eggs
1 tablespoon Dijon mustard
2 tablespoons water
1 pound skinless white fish fillets (such as cod or
  haddock), cut into 3-inch pieces (should be
  about 7 pieces)
1 lemon, cut into wedges

Instructions

1. Lightly grease a baking sheet that has sides. Preheat oven to
   450°F. Peel potatoes and cut in half, and then cut each half into
   8 wedges. In a bowl, toss the potatoes with the olive oil, paprika,
   salt, and pepper. Place potatoes on the baking sheet in a single
   layer. Bake in preheated oven for 15 minutes.

2. Meanwhile, prepare the fish. Place the melba toast in a resealable
   plastic bag and pound with a mallet or the back of a heavy spoon
   to crush. There will be some pieces that remain large (the size of a
   pebble); this is okay as it adds to the texture once baked.

3. Place the crushed melba toast on a plate. In a shallow bowl, whisk
   together the eggs, Dijon mustard, and water.

4. Season the fish with salt and pepper to taste. Dip the fish on
   both sides with egg mixture and then press to coat with crumbs,
   turning to coat both sides.

5. After the potatoes have cooked for 15 minutes, use a spatula and
   push them to one side of the pan. Place fish in the pan, making
   sure they do not touch and return pan to oven. Bake for another
   15 minutes, until the fish is crisp and firm to the touch.

6. Serve immediately with a lemon wedge.

Lady and Tramp's
Cartwheels with Tomato Sauce

Ingredients

4 ½ tablespoons olive oil
1 medium onion, finely chopped
1 medium green bell pepper, finely chopped
1 small carrot, grated
1 clove garlic, minced
4 ½ cups (about 42 ounces) crushed
   tomatoes in puree
2 teaspoons dried basil

1 teaspoon dried oregano
½ scant teaspoon salt, plus 2 teaspoons for the
   cooking water
Freshly ground pepper to taste
½ pound smoked turkey sausage, quartered
   lengthwise and diced
¾ pound cartwheel pasta
Grated Parmesan cheese for garnish

Instructions

1. Heat 2 ½ tablespoons of the olive oil in a medium saucepan. Add the onion, pepper, and carrot. Partially cover the pan, then sweat the vegetables over moderate heat for about 8 minutes, stirring occasionally, until the onion is translucent.
2. Add the garlic and cook for 30 seconds.
3. Add the tomatoes, basil, oregano, salt, pepper, and sausage (note: smoked sausage is precooked; do not substitute raw sausage). Cover the pan and cook the sauce at a gentle simmer for 15 to 20 minutes, stirring occasionally.
4. While the sauce simmers, bring 4 to 5 quarts of water to a boil and add 1 tablespoon of olive oil and 2 teaspoons of salt. Gradually add the cartwheel pasta and cook according to the package directions.
5. Drain the cooked pasta and transfer it to a large serving bowl. Drizzle with 1 tablespoon of olive oil and toss briefly. Spoon one third of the sauce over the pasta and toss again. Ladle on the rest of the hot sauce, sprinkle with Parmesan cheese, and serve immediately.

Serving: 1 ¼ cups
Calories: 329
Total Fat: 13g
Total Carbohydrate: 43g
Fiber: 3g
Protein: 12g
Carbohydrate Choice: 3

Gluten-free note: prepare with gluten-free pasta (carbohydrate amount will vary).

Lady and Tramp's Tip: This is one pasta dinner to bark about! Pups can measure out the spices, stir the sauce, and sprinkle on the Parmesan cheese.

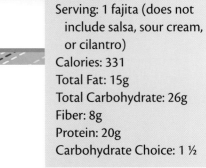

Donald's Tip: Have dinner south of the border with these chicken fajitas! Mama and Papa should grill the chicken, but *los niños* will enjoy setting out the toppings and rolling their fajitas!

Serving: 1 fajita (does not include salsa, sour cream, or cilantro)
Calories: 331
Total Fat: 15g
Total Carbohydrate: 26g
Fiber: 8g
Protein: 20g
Carbohydrate Choice: 1 ½

Gluten-free note: serve with corn tortillas (carbohydrate amount will vary).

Donald's
Chicken Fajitas

Ingredients

1 ripe avocado, cut into chunks, with 1 teaspoon
   of lime juice tossed in
Salsa
Sour cream
Fresh cilantro, chopped
4 teaspoons ground cumin
4 teaspoons chili powder

1 teaspoon dried oregano
½ teaspoon salt
2 boneless, skinless chicken breasts, cut in half
1 small red or yellow pepper, sliced
1 onion, sliced
2 teaspoons olive oil
4 8-inch flour tortillas

Instructions

1. Place your toppings (avocado, salsa, sour cream, and cilantro leaves) in separate bowls and set them on your table.
2. Next, make the rub. Combine the cumin, chili powder, oregano, and salt in a shallow bowl. Lightly rub the spices into the chicken with your fingertips until the meat is coated on all sides. Heat your grill to medium. Grill the chicken on both sides, just until cooked through, about 8 minutes. Remove from the heat, slice thinly, and set it on a platter.
3. While the chicken is cooking, toss the pepper and onion in the olive oil. Set them on the grill, using a vegetable screen, if desired, and cook for 5 to 8 minutes, turning once. Remove from the heat and set on the platter with the chicken.
4. Place the tortillas on the grill for 5 to 7 seconds on each side, turning with tongs, until hot. Set out the grilled chicken, pepper, and onion with the toppings and tortillas. Let guests assemble and roll their own fajitas.

SNACKS & SWEETS

Pocahontas's
Peanut Butter Trail Mix Balls

Ingredients

1 cup peanut butter
1 cup honey
3 cups old-fashioned oats
½ cup ground flaxseed
1 cup chocolate chips
½ cup chopped nuts of your choice
½ cup dried fruit of your choice

Instructions

1. Mix together 1 cup peanut butter and 1 cup honey until smooth. Gradually add in 3 cups of old-fashioned oats and ½ cup ground flaxseed. Add 1 cup chocolate chips and 1 cup any combination of nuts and soft dried fruit (try ½ cup coarsely chopped peanuts and ¼ cup each of raisins and dried cranberries) and mix gently in your stand mixer or smush together by hand.
2. Roll into Ping-Pong–size balls and, for maximum presentation value, put in paper mini-muffin cups. You can eat them right away, but they'll be less sticky after a night in the fridge. They freeze well too, layered on wax paper in an airtight container.

Serving: 1 ball
Calories: 133
Total Fat: 6g
Total Carbohydrate: 16g
Fiber: 2g
Protein: 3g
Carbohydrate Choice: 1

Gluten-free note: prepare
with gluten-free oats.

Pocahontas's Tip: When you're outdoors all day long, it's easy to work up an appetite! Young members of the tribe will love digging their hands into the dough and rolling it into balls.

Belle's Tip: Some people might say that delicious, healthy brownies are a myth or a fairy tale, but that simply isn't true! While Mom or Dad melts the butter, kids can measure and mix the dry ingredients.

Serving: 1 piece
Calories: 85
Total Fat: 4g
Total Carbohydrate: 11g
Fiber: 1g
Protein: 1g
Carbohydrate Choice: 1

Belle's
Better Brownies

Ingredients

½ cup flour
⅓ cup cocoa powder
½ teaspoon baking powder
⅛ teaspoon salt
4 tablespoons butter
2 squares (2 ounces) bittersweet chocolate, chopped

1 large egg
2 large egg whites
1 cup sugar
1 tablespoon canola oil
2 teaspoons vanilla extract
1 teaspoon instant espresso or coffee powder (optional)

Instructions

1. Heat the oven to 350°F. Lightly coat an 8-inch-square pan with cooking spray. In a medium bowl, whisk together the flour, cocoa powder, baking powder, and salt. Set the mixture aside.

2. Heat the butter in a small saucepan until just melted, being careful not to burn it. Remove the pan from the heat. Add the chopped chocolate, stirring until it is melted. Let the chocolate mixture cool until it's tepid.

3. In a medium bowl, lightly whisk the egg and egg whites just until combined. Whisk in the cooled chocolate mixture, sugar, oil, vanilla extract, and espresso powder (if you're using it) until smooth. Stir in the flour mixture, but do not overmix the batter.

4. Use a rubber spatula to scrape the batter into the prepared pan and smooth the top. Bake the brownies on the center oven rack until the edges begin to pull away from the sides of the pan, about 25 minutes. The brownies will look underbaked (a cake tester will come out with a few moist crumbs), but they will set up more as they cool. Place the pan on a wire cake rack to let the brownies cool, then slice the batch into 24 pieces.

Pumbaa's
Black Bean Salsa

Ingredients

2 medium-size Roma tomatoes
½ medium-size red onion
3 scallions
1 (15 ½-ounce) can black beans, drained and rinsed
1 ½ tablespoons taco seasoning mix
2 tablespoons sour cream or plain yogurt

Instructions

1. Using a small knife, halve each tomato. Cut away the stem area, then cut the two halves in half. Over the sink or a small bowl, squeeze the tomato pieces as you would a sponge to force out the seeds and water. Use a knife or hand-powered food chopper to dice the tomatoes. Transfer to a large bowl.

2. Dice the red onion and add it to the bowl. Finely chop the scallions and add them to the bowl, along with the beans.

3. Sprinkle on the taco seasoning and lightly toss the mixture until evenly blended. Spoon in the sour cream or yogurt and toss again until the ingredients are fully coated.

Serving: ½ cup
Calories: 71
Total Fat: 1g
Total Carbohydrate: 11g
Fiber: 4g
Protein: 5g
Carbohydrate Choice: 1

Gluten-free note: prepare with gluten-free taco seasoning and yogurt.

Pumbaa's Tip: Warthogs and meerkats go wild for this salsa! Parents and big kids can chop the veggies, while small fries drain and rinse the beans.

Minnie's
Frozen Fruit Bites

Ingredients

12 vanilla wafer cookies
½ cup vanilla yogurt
½ cup Neufchâtel cream cheese, softened
1 teaspoon lemon juice
1 teaspoon honey
Sliced kiwi, strawberries, or whole blueberries

Instructions

1. Place liners in a mini-cupcake pan. Put a wafer cookie, flat side up, in the bottom of each well.
2. In a medium-size bowl, whisk together the yogurt, cream cheese, lemon juice, and honey until smooth. Spoon 1 heaping tablespoon on top of each cookie, then top the mixture with the fruit.
3. Cover the pan with plastic wrap, then place it in the freezer until the fruit bites are firm, about 1 to 1½ hours. Remove the tray from the freezer 15 to 25 minutes before serving.

Serving: 1 cookie
Calories: 68
Total Fat: 4g
Total Carbohydrate: 7g
Fiber: 0g
Protein: 2g
Carbohydrate Choice: ½

Minnie's Tip: The only thing more fun than making these cookies is sharing them with friends! With a parent's supervision, kids can follow this recipe from beginning to end.

Pooh's
Honey Apple Cake

Ingredients

CAKE
4 large eggs
¾ cup honey
1 ¼ cups sugar
⅓ cup canola oil
¼ cup water
2 ¼ cups unbleached flour
2 teaspoons baking powder
¾ teaspoon baking soda
1 teaspoon cinnamon

½ teaspoon nutmeg
½ teaspoon allspice
½ teaspoon salt
2 cups apple (such as Cortland, Macoun, or McIntosh), peeled and finely chopped
1 cup walnuts, finely chopped

TOPPING
⅓ cup honey
¼ cup walnuts, finely chopped

Instructions

1. Heat the oven to 300°F, then generously butter a 10-inch Bundt pan. In a large bowl, combine the eggs, honey, sugar, oil, and water, beating with an electric mixer until well blended, about 3 minutes.
2. In another large bowl, whisk together the flour, baking powder, baking soda, cinnamon, nutmeg, allspice, and salt. Add the apples and walnuts and toss to coat evenly.
3. Add the liquid ingredients to the dry mixture and beat until smooth, about 2 minutes. Scrape the batter into the prepared pan.
4. Bake for 70 to 75 minutes or until a knife inserted into the center of the cake comes out clean. Cool the cake on a rack for 5 minutes, then invert the pan onto a plate to remove the cake. Top the cake by spreading on the ⅓ cup of honey and sprinkle on the ¼ cup of walnuts, pressing them down gently with your fingers. Allow the cake to cool completely before serving.

Serving: 1 piece
Calories: 213
Total Fat: 8g
Total Carbohydrate: 33g
Fiber: 1g
Protein: 3g
Carbohydrate Choice: 2

Pooh's Tip: This honey-covered cake will put a rumbly in everyone's tumbly! Piglets can measure out all the ingredients and spread on the honey topping.

Chip 'n' Dale's Tip: It's hard not to squirrel away these nut-tastic snacks! Junior chipmunks can get artistic and drizzle the chocolate glaze over the chilled clusters.

Serving: 1 cluster
Calories: 99
Total Fat: 7g
Total Carbohydrate: 8g
Fiber: 1g
Protein: 1g
Carbohydrate Choice: ½

Gluten-free

Chip 'n' Dale's
Crunchy Nut Clusters

Ingredients

CANDY CUPS
2 ⅔ cups sweetened, flaked coconut
2 cups pecans or 1 (6-ounce) jar macadamia nuts, chopped
2 ⅔ cups white or semisweet chocolate chips

GLAZE
⅓ cup white chocolate (melted with ½ tablespoon vegetable shortening) or ⅓ cup semisweet chocolate

Instructions

1. Line 4 miniature muffin pans with candy cups; set them aside. Heat the oven to 350°F. Spread the coconut and nuts on separate cookie sheets. Bake each until golden brown, about 9 minutes for the nuts and 10 for the coconut, stirring every few minutes to keep them from burning. Let them cool.

2. Combine the toasted coconut and nuts in a medium-size bowl. Melt the chocolate chips—white or semisweet—in the microwave according to the package directions. Add the melted chocolate to the coconut mixture; stir well. Drop the mixture by heaping teaspoonfuls into the candy cups. Chill until set, about 45 minutes.

3. Melt the remaining chocolate according to the package directions. Pour the contents into a resealable plastic bag. Snip off a small corner of the bag, then drizzle the chocolate over the clusters. Chill until the glaze is set, about 15 minutes. Store in an airtight container in the refrigerator.

Pinocchio's
Peach Raspberry Cobbler

FRUIT FILLING
4 cups peeled, sliced ripe peaches
1 ½ cups fresh raspberries
½ cup sugar
1 tablespoon lemon juice
1 tablespoon flour

COBBLER TOPPING
1 ⅓ cups flour
¼ cup, plus 1 tablespoon sugar
1 ½ teaspoons baking powder
¼ teaspoon salt
4 tablespoons cold, unsalted butter, cut into ¼–inch pieces
⅓ cup milk
⅓ cup sour cream or plain yogurt
1 large egg
½ teaspoon vanilla extract
¼ teaspoon ground cinnamon

1. Heat the oven to 400°F. Butter or coat a 10-inch pie dish with cooking spray and set it aside.
2. In a large mixing bowl, combine the peaches, raspberries, sugar, lemon juice, and flour. Toss well, then transfer the mixture to the pie dish. Bake on the center oven shelf for 20 minutes.
3. For the cobbler topping, sift the flour, ¼ cup of sugar, baking powder, and salt into a large mixing bowl. Add the butter and cut or rub it into the dry ingredients with a pastry blender or your fingers until it is broken into small bits.
4. In a separate bowl, whisk together the milk, sour cream or yogurt, egg, and vanilla extract until blended. Make a well in the dry ingredients, then pour in the liquid, stirring just until moistened.
5. When the fruit filling is done, remove it from the oven. Use a tablespoon to spoon the topping here and there over the fruit so it will look like cobblestones when it's baked, covering as much of the fruit as possible.
6. Mix the remaining 1 tablespoon of sugar with the cinnamon in a small bowl, then sprinkle evenly over the topping.
7. Bake the cobbler for 20 minutes or until golden brown. Cool for 10 to 15 minutes before serving.

Serving: ⅛ of cobbler
Calories: 285
Total Fat: 9g
Total Carbohydrate: 45g
Fiber: 3g
Protein: 5g
Carbohydrate Choice: 3

Pinocchio's Tip: This is no lie: peach and raspberry cobbler is the perfect summer dessert! Little ones can pitch in with almost every step—from measuring the ingredients to spooning the topping onto the fruit.

Prince Eric's
Deviled R-egg-atta

Ingredients

12 hard-boiled eggs
2 teaspoons Dijon mustard
2 teaspoons vinegar (white or cider)
¼ cup mayonnaise
2 red, orange, yellow, or green bell peppers
Paprika

Instructions

1. Peel the eggs, then slice each one in half to make boats. Place the yolks in a medium-size bowl and mash them with a fork. Add the mustard and the vinegar, then add the mayonnaise, stirring until the consistency is smooth but not soupy.
2. Next, make the sails. To do this, cut each pepper into 1-inch-wide strips, then cut the strips into 1-inch squares and slice each square in half diagonally.
3. Fill the egg-white halves with the yolk mixture. Stick the sail upright into the filling and sprinkle with paprika.

Serving: 2 egg halves
Calories: 116
Total Fat: 9g
Total Carbohydrate: 1g
Fiber: 0g
Protein: 6g
Carbohydrate Choice: 0

Gluten-free

Prince Eric's Tip: For a shipshape snack, deviled egg sailboats are right on course. To help create them, young skippers can peel the hard-boiled eggs, mash the yolks, and set the sails!

Lilo's
Summer Fruit Pizza

Ingredients

1 pound purchased pizza dough, or your favorite homemade recipe

1 tablespoon melted butter

2 tablespoons sugar

1 (8-ounce) package low-fat cream cheese at room temperature

¼ cup sugar

1 teaspoon finely grated orange zest

½ teaspoon vanilla extract

Assorted fruit (such as blueberries, banana slices, mandarin orange sections, seedless grapes, kiwi fruit slices, and strawberry halves)

Instructions

1. Heat the oven to 400°F.
2. Spread the dough in an ungreased 12-inch pizza pan. Brush on the butter and sprinkle on the 2 tablespoons of sugar. Bake the crust until it is golden brown, 12 to 15 minutes. Cool the crust on a wire rack.
3. In a medium-size bowl, combine the frosting ingredients with a rubber spatula. Stir until smooth.
4. Spread the frosting over the cooled crust. Gently press in the fruit.

Serving: 1 slice
Calories: 180
Total Fat: 4g
Total Carbohydrate: 28g
Fiber: 3g
Protein: 5g
Carbohydrate Choice: 2

Gluten-free note: prepare with gluten-free pizza crust (carbohydrate amount will vary).

Lilo's Tip: For a hint of Hawaii on your pizza, add some pineapple! Kids—and aliens—can use their favorite fruits to turn this dessert into a work of art.

Lumiere's Tip: If you are having guests, this sweet treat is just the thing to serve. Pint-size chefs can use their hands to work the dough, and then they can zest the lemons.

Serving: 1 2-inch square
Calories: 157
Total Fat: 7g
Total Carbohydrate: 22g
Fiber: 1g
Protein: 2g
Carbohydrate Choice: 1 ½

Lumiere's
Luscious Lemon Bars

Ingredients

SHORTBREAD
¾ cup butter, at room temperature
1 ½ cups all-purpose flour
½ cup confectioners' sugar

FILLING
2 lemons
4 eggs
1 ½ cups sugar
¼ cup all-purpose flour

Instructions

1. Heat the oven to 350°F. For the shortbread crust, use your fingertips to work the butter, flour, and confectioners' sugar in a large bowl until the mixture holds together. Transfer the dough to an ungreased 9x13-inch pan and press it into the pan. Bake for 20 minutes, or until the edges begin to brown.

2. While the shortbread is baking, make the lemon filling. Wash and dry the lemons, then grate the rinds using the small holes on your grater (you will need 2 tablespoons of zest). Slice each lemon in half and squeeze the juice into a measuring cup until you have ⅓ cup. Remove any seeds.

3. In a large mixing bowl, whisk together the eggs and sugar. Whisk in the flour. Stir in the lemon zest and juice. When the shortbread has baked, pour the filling over it and return the pan to the oven for another 20 to 25 minutes or until the filling no longer jiggles and the edges are lightly browned. (Test by inserting a knife in the middle.) Cool and dust with confectioners' sugar. Refrigerate any leftovers.

Acknowledgments

The producers of this book would like to thank the staff of *Disney FamilyFun*, who created the recipes and photos that fill this book. A special thank-you goes out to Deanna Cook and Jean Cranston.

Copyright © 2011 Disney Enterprises, Inc. Published by Disney Editions, an imprint of Disney Book Group. All rights reserved. No part of this book may be reproduced or transmitted in any form or by any means, electronic or mechanical, including photocopying, recording, or by any information storage and retrieval system, without written permission from the publisher. For information address Disney Editions, 114 Fifth Avenue, New York, New York 10011-5690.

Editorial Director: Wendy Lefkon
Associate Editor: Jessica Ward
Managing Editor: Jennifer Eastwood
Design Manager: Winnie Ho

Disney FamilyFun is a division of Disney Publishing Worldwide. For more great ideas and to subscribe to *Disney FamilyFun* magazine, visit FamilyFun.com or call 1-800-289-4849.
ISBN 978-1-4231-2679-9   G942-9090-6-12341   First Edition   10 9 8 7 6 5 4 3 2
Visit www.disneybooks.com

HI 70282   0711   PRINTED IN USA.   LILLY IS A REGISTERED TRADEMARK OF ELI LILLY AND COMPANY.
NOT FOR RESALE

Looking for tips on family life with type 1 diabetes?
Visit www.family.com/type1

D23
The Official Community for Disney Fans
Disney.com/D23

SUSTAINABLE FORESTRY INITIATIVE   Certified Sourcing
www.sfiprogram.org
SFI-00993
For Text Only